Walt Disney's
CINDERELLA

A GOLDEN BOOK • NEW YORK
Western Publishing Company, Inc., Racine, Wisconsin 53404

Once upon a time in a faraway kingdom, there lived a widowed gentleman and his lovely daughter, Ella.

Ella was a beautiful girl. She had golden hair, and her eyes were as blue as forget-me-nots.

The gentleman was a kind and devoted father, and he gave Ella everything her heart desired. But he felt she needed a mother. So he married again, choosing for his wife a woman who had two daughters. Their names were Anastasia and Drizella.

Sadly, the gentleman soon died. Then the stepmother's true nature was revealed. Only interested in her ugly, selfish daughters, she spent every penny on ribbons, laces, and jewelry for them. She gave nothing to Ella.

The stepmother fired the butlers and maids, and made Ella a servant. She gave Ella a little room in the attic, old rags to wear, and all the housework to do. Soon everyone called her Cinderella, because she got so covered with cinders from cleaning the fireplaces.

But Cinderella stayed cheerful, for she had many friends. The old horse and Bruno the dog loved her. The mice loved her, too. She protected them from her stepmother's nasty cat, Lucifer, and made them tiny suits of clothes. Two of her favorite mice, Gus and Jaq, always tried to help her with the housework.

Cinderella was kind to everyone—even to Lucifer. But Lucifer only took advantage of her kindness.

Lucifer liked to get Cinderella in trouble. One morning, he chased Gus under a teacup on Anastasia's breakfast tray. She screamed when she found Gus, and blamed Cinderella.

"As punishment for playing this joke," the stepmother said to Cinderella, "you will wash the windows, scrub the terrace, and sweep the halls. And don't forget the sewing and the laundry."

"But I just finished..." Cinderella cried.

"Then do them again!" snapped the evil woman.

In another part of the kingdom, the King was worrying about his son.

"It's time the Prince got married!" he told the Grand Duke. "I need grandchildren!"

"But, Sire," said the Grand Duke, "he must fall in love first."

"No buts about it! We'll have a ball. It will be very romantic. He'll fall in love!"

"But, Sire, it's not that easy," argued the Grand Duke.

"It can't fail!" the King shouted. "We'll have the ball tonight! Send out the invitations!"

There was great excitement in Cinderella's house when the invitation arrived.

"By royal command," the stepmother read from the official-looking note, "every girl in the kingdom is invited to a ball in honor of the Prince."

"Why, that means I can go, too," Cinderella said.

"Well, yes...I suppose it does," the stepmother replied with a sly smile. "But *only* if you get all your work done, and *only* if you have something suitable to wear."

Cinderella had hoped to fix her old party dress, but Anastasia and Drizella wanted her to help them, instead.

"Cinderella! Iron my petticoat!" they ordered. "Cinderella! Clean my shoes! Cinderella! Draw my bath and curl my hair!"

The stepmother kept her busy, too. "Clean the chimney! Dust the parlor! Mend these buttonholes! Polish the silver!"

Cinderella worked hard all day long. When she finally came back to her little attic room, it was almost time to leave for the ball. And her dress wasn't ready!

But her loyal friends, the mice, had taken care of everything.
While Cinderella was working, so were they! Dodging Lucifer's
sharp claws, Gus and Jaq managed to find ribbons, sashes,
ruffles, and bows. The mice sewed them to her party dress.
It looked beautiful.

When Drizella saw Cinderella, she shrieked, "Those are my
ribbons! Give them back!"

"That's my sash," shouted Anastasia. "You little sneak!"

The stepsisters snatched and grabbed until the dress was in
shreds.

"That's enough, girls," said the stepmother. "Come along to
the ball."

Cinderella ran into the garden. She wept and **wept. The old** horse, the mice, and Bruno the dog stood by helplessly.

Suddenly a hush fell over the garden, and a cloud of lights began to twinkle and glow around Cinderella's head.

"Come on, dry those tears," came a gentle voice. Then a small woman appeared in the cloud. "You can't go to the ball looking like that. Now, where's my magic wand?"

"Magic wand?" gasped Cinderella. "Are you my..."

"Fairy godmother," the woman replied, pulling her magic wand out of thin air.

"What we need is a pumpkin," she continued. "Watch this!

"Salaga doola, menchika boola, bibbidi, bobbidi, boo!
Put 'em together and what have you got?
Bibbidi, bobbidi, boo!"

As she sang the words, a cloud of sparkles floated across the garden. A pumpkin rose up and swelled into an elegant coach, the mice turned into horses, the old horse became a coachman, and Bruno became a footman.

"Now off you go, deary," said the woman.

"But my dress..." said Cinderella.

"You look lovely," the fairy godmother said absentmindedly. Then she took a second look. "Good heavens! You can't go to the ball in that! Hmmm, let's see now..."

With a wave of her wand, she turned Cinderella's rags into an exquisite gown. On Cinderella's feet were tiny glass slippers.

"Remember," the fairy godmother said, "you must leave the ball at midnight. That's when the spell will be broken and all will be as it was before."

When Cinderella arrived at the ball, the Prince was yawning with boredom. Drizella and Anastasia had just been introduced to him. Then he caught sight of Cinderella.

Ignoring everything around him, the Prince walked over to her. He kissed Cinderella's hand, and asked her to dance. They swirled off across the ballroom.

The Prince never left Cinderella's side. They danced every
dance together. As everyone watched them, the lights dimmed
and sweet music floated out into the summer night.

"Good," said the King with a contented smile. "Notify me the
minute he proposes. I'm going to bed."

And then Cinderella heard the clock begin to chime.

"Oh, no!" she gasped. "It's midnight. I must go!"

"Wait! Come back!" called the Prince. But Cinderella was
already running out of the ballroom.

Cinderella hurried down the palace steps. Tripping for a moment, she lost one of the glass slippers, but she had no time to pick it up. She leapt into the waiting coach.

As soon as the coach went through the gates, the magic spell broke. Cinderella found herself standing by the side of the road, dressed in her old rags. Next to her was a pumpkin, four mice, an old horse, and Bruno the dog. But on her foot, she still wore the other glass slipper.

The next day, the stepmother told the girls that the Grand Duke was coming to see them. "He's searching the kingdom," she said, "for the young lady whose foot fits the glass slipper. The King has said that whoever she is, she will marry the Prince."

Cinderella smiled, and left the room humming. Her stepmother, hearing Cinderella humming the very waltz that had been played at the ball, became suspicious. She followed Cinderella up to her room, and quickly locked the girl inside. Slipping the key into her pocket, the stepmother hurried off to greet the Grand Duke.

Gus and Jaq had a plan to help Cinderella. While Anastasia
and Drizella each tried to squeeze their big feet into the
little glass slipper, the two mice sneaked up the back of the
stepmother's chair. Carefully, Gus lowered Jaq into her pocket,
and they got hold of the key. They tugged the heavy key up the
stairs, and unlocked the door. Cinderella went downstairs to try
on the glass slipper.

When Cinderella came into the room, the Grand Duke's eyes lit up.

"Your Grace," she said, "may I try on the slipper?"

The wicked stepmother fumed with anger. She tripped the pageboy who was holding the glass slipper. It fell to the floor and broke into a thousand pieces. The Grand Duke was horrified, but not Cinderella.

"Don't worry," she said, reaching into her pocket. "I have the other one right here."

She put on the slipper, and, of course, it fit perfectly.

From that moment on, everything was a dream come true.
Cinderella went off to the palace with the happy Grand Duke.
The Prince was overjoyed to see her again, and so was the King.
She and the Prince were soon married.

In her happiness, Cinderella didn't forget about her friends—
Bruno the dog, the old horse, the birds, Gus and Jaq, and other
mice. They all moved into the castle with her.

Everyone in the kingdom was delighted with the Prince's new
bride. Cinderella and the Prince lived happily ever after!